SNOW DOG

Illustrated by Sami Sweeten

malorie
blackman

CORGI PUPS

www.randomhousechildrens.co.uk

SNOW DOG
A CORGI PUPS BOOK 978 0 552 54703 1

First published in Great Britain by Corgi Pups,
an imprint of Random House Children's Books
A Random House Group Company

Corgi Pups edition published 2001
This edition published 2010

11

The Random House Group Limited supports The Forest Stewardship
Council® (FSC®), the leading international forest-certification organisation.
Our books carrying the FSC label are printed on FSC®-certified paper.
FSC is the only forest-certification scheme supported by the leading
environmental organisations, including Greenpeace. Our
paper procurement policy can be found at
www.randomhouse.co.uk/environment

MIX
Paper from
responsible sources
FSC® C016897

Set in Bembo

Corgi Pups are published by Random House Children's Books,
61–63 Uxbridge Road, London W5 5SA

www.randomhousechildrens.co.uk
www.randomhouse.co.uk

Addresses for companies within The Random House Group Limited
can be found at: www.randomhouse.co.uk/offices.htm

THE RANDOM HOUSE GROUP Limited Reg. No. 954009

A CIP catalogue record for this book is available
from the British Library.

Printed and bound in Great Britain by
Clays Ltd, St Ives plc

✳ CONTENTS ✳

Series consultant: Prue Goodwin
Lecturer in Literacy and Children's Books,
University of Reading

*For Neil and Lizzy, with love,
and for Donnika — as promised!*

Chapter One
Grandad's Idea

Nicky lived with her mum and
her dad in a beautiful house
with lots of rooms. The house
had a big garden at the front
and an even bigger garden at the
back. But Nicky was miserable.

She didn't mind not having any brothers or sisters, but there was one thing she wanted more than anything else in the world.

"Mum, *please* can I have a dog?"

"You must be joking, sweet pea," sniffed Nicky's mum as she hunted for her handbag.

"Why not?"

"Because a dog would make a mess of our carpets," said Nicky's mum, as she searched in her handbag for her front door keys.

"We could make a kennel for it in our back garden," Nicky tried.

"In the garden?" Nicky's mum was horrified. "Where it could dig up my tulips and my pansies and my roses? Are you crazy? I don't think so, poppet."

And Mum rushed off to work.

"Dad, can I have a dog *please*?" Nicky pleaded, as Dad came downstairs.

"I'm afraid not, precious."

"But why not?" Nicky was trying not to cry.

"Because, my apple dumpling, your mum and I work during the day and you're at school, so who would look after it?" said Dad.

9

"I would when I got home from school," Nicky replied eagerly. "No, honey muffin. Dogs need to be exercised regularly – through rain or shine, snow or hail. You're too young to take a dog for regular walks and your mum and I are too busy. It just wouldn't work." Dad rummaged through the notes and letters on the hall table looking for the shopping list. "Ah, there it is!"

Dad tucked the list into his shirt pocket.

"Couldn't we try, just for a while?" Nicky pleaded.

"No, angel lips. I'm sorry, but no." And Dad headed out of the door to do the shopping.

Tears started to stream down Nicky's face. Grandad, who had been watching everything from the living room, came out into the hall holding the biggest hankie she had ever seen. Grandad's hankie was almost the size of a tablecloth!

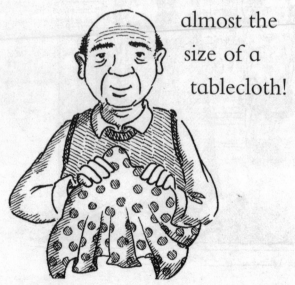

"Never mind, Nicky. Use my
hankie to dry your eyes. Don't
worry, it's clean!" And Grandad
dropped the whole thing down
on Nicky's head. It covered her
face like a huge and very floppy
hat.

"Grandad!" Nicky laughed as she pulled it off. "I haven't got twenty eyes spread out all over my head!"

"That's my girl," Grandad grinned. "Cheer up, treasure."

"Oh Grandad, I wish you lived closer so that we could see you more often. Then maybe Mum and Dad would let me have a dog – if you could be here to look after it," Nicky sighed.

"Don't worry, sweetie. Dry your eyes and I'll tell you about my idea."

"What idea?" asked Nicky, wiping her eyes.

"Do you really and truly want a dog?" asked Grandad.

"Mum and Dad won't let me have one." Nicky  sniffed, her eyes itching with fresh tears.

"They won't buy one for you, but I know how we could get you a dog of your very own." Grandad's eyes were twinkling.

"How?"

"We could make one!" said Grandad.

16

Chapter Two
Waiting

"Make one?" Nicky stared at
her grandad.

"That's right."

"How on earth can we make
our own dog?" asked Nicky.

"Come with me." Grandad
led the way into the living
room. "Now then, where did I
put it?"

"Put what?"

"My bag," said Grandad
looking around.

"It's over there, next to the telly." Nicky wondered how Grandad could miss it! His bag was gigantic and Mum and Dad were always complaining that it looked like Grandad was carrying a huge scatter cushion on his shoulder.

"Right then, stand back!"
Grandad bent down and buried
his head in the bag. It looked
like he was diving right into it.
Nicky watched as Grandad
started throwing out all kinds of

20

things, like a yellow lampshade
and an electric kettle and a
half-eaten packet of chocolate
biscuits. Several books, a few
CDs and a computer keyboard
flew across the room after the
biscuits.

"Ah! Here it is!" exclaimed
Grandad at last. "The very thing."

"What is it?" Nicky couldn't
resist going closer to see.

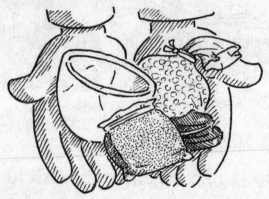

"It's a snow dome kit. It's got
a dome and the base and glitter
and bits of plastic we can use for
snow and it's got extra-special
clay that we can use to make
your dog."

"What's extra-special about it?" asked Nicky.

"I found this clay at the end of the most beautiful rainbow I've ever seen in my life," said Grandad. "I dug it up myself. And everyone knows rainbows are made of wishes and are very special. So any dog made with this clay will be extra-special. Maybe even magic . . ."

"A clay dog isn't the same as having a real dog." Nicky sighed.

"We'll see," winked Grandad. "We'll see."

For the next hour, Grandad and Nicky sat at the table making a snow dome dog.

Nicky made the body and the face and Grandad made the tail and the legs. Nicky gave her dog big, floppy ears and, very carefully, she turned up the corners of the puppy's mouth. And she turned his tail up too, to show that he was wagging it.

"That's better. He looks like a happy dog now." Nicky sat back, satisfied.

At last it was finished.

"Now we have to bake it until it's quite hard," said Grandad. "And then we can paint it."

When at last the dog had
baked and was cool enough to
paint, Nicky did that all by
herself. She painted her dog a
golden brown with dark brown
eyes and silver paws.

"Perfect!" said Grandad.
"Now we just have to wait for
the paint to dry,"

As soon as the
paint was dry,
Nicky very
carefully
attached the
puppy to the base of the dome.
Grandad filled the glass dome
with water and asked, "Shall we
put in the snow or some glitter?"

"The snow," Nicky replied at once.

"Snow it is then," said Grandad. And he tipped the packet of white plastic snow into the water in the dome.

Grandad turned the base upside down and screwed it onto the dome, before clicking it into place.

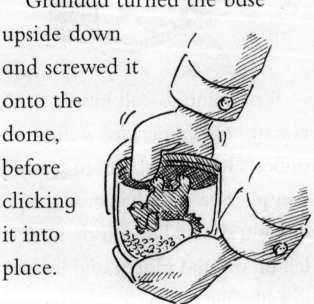

He turned the dome the right
way round and handed it over
to his granddaughter. "And here
it is! Your very own snow dog!"

"I'm going to call him
Harry," Nicky decided with a
smile. "Hello, Harry. Aren't you
pretty?" She gave her snow
dome a shake. The plastic snow
fell all around Harry and looked
just like real snow.

"Can I take him into the garden?" Nicky asked.

"Of course. Take a jumper though. It's a bit chilly out there."

"Chilly! It's baking out there!" Nicky glanced out of the window. There wasn't a cloud in the summer sky and the sun was blazing down.

"Jumper, please!" Grandad insisted.

Nicky ran upstairs to get a jumper. She tied it around her waist rather than put it on.

Grandad might be cold, but she certainly wasn't. She ran back downstairs to the kitchen.

"Out you go then," nodded Grandad when he saw Nicky had her jumper. "I'll call you when it's lunch-time."

So off Nicky went. She sat on
her swing, twisting her legs this
way, then that. She shook the
snow dome again.

Harry was indeed the most
beautiful dog in the world. Nicky
sighed, a deep, unhappy sigh.

"I wish you were real, then I could play in there with you," she whispered.

A very strange thing began to happen. The snow dome grew colder and colder as Nicky held it, until it felt like she was holding a snowball at the North Pole! But that was impossible. It was the middle of summer and the sun was shining like a brand new coin.

Nicky put the snow
dome down on the
grass and blew on
her fingers. They were
almost numb. She frowned down
at the dome. What was going on?

"Oh my goodness!" Nicky
exclaimed.

Harry was wagging his tail. He
was actually wagging his tail! And
now he was barking. A very tiny,
faint sound but it was definitely
a bark.

Chapter Three
Harry

Nicky blinked once, blinked twice and then it happened. The third time she blinked, she opened her eyes to find herself standing in front of a real, live, furry Harry. And there was snow falling all around them.

"How woof-onderful!" said Harry. "You've come to play with me. I hoped you would!"

"You can talk too?" Nicky asked, amazed.

"Of course," Harry said. "All dogs talk! At least, they do in here. Isn't it woof-onderful?"

Nicky couldn't believe it. She
was *inside* the dome and just a bit
bigger than Harry. Grandad had
said the clay might be magic.
Nicky looked around. What a
beautiful place! Somewhere,
far off in the distance, lights

twinkled just like fairy lights on a
Christmas tree.

And here and there were fir
and pine trees, swaying to and fro
in the wind as if they were
waving at Nicky to welcome her.
And the air smelt crisp and clean.

Nicky took a delighted deep
breath. There was just one thing
wrong.

"Brrrr! It's freezing in here!"
"Put on your jumper then,"
Harry suggested.

Nicky had completely for-
gotten about the jumper tied
around her waist. She untied it
and quickly pulled it on. Much,
much better! She wasn't the least
bit cold now. Funny it should be
so cold when the snow was only
plastic. Nicky put out her hand.

Snow fell on it, melting away
just like real snowflakes.

From the outside, the dome
looked like plastic and clay and
glass, but on the inside everything
was real. What a weird, wonderful
place!

"So what're we going to play
first?"

"Play?"

"Well, that is why you made me, isn't it? So we can play together?" said Harry.

Nicky nodded. She wasn't sure how to play with a snow dog but she was certainly willing to learn.

"Throw a snowball and I'll fetch it!" said Harry.

"But it'll melt in your mouth," Nicky laughed.

"Try it," Harry insisted.

So Nicky picked up a handful
of snow and squeezed it together
until it was ball-shaped, then she
threw it as hard as she could.

In a flash, Harry was off chasing after it. And to Nicky's surprise, he came trotting back to her with the snowball still intact in his mouth.

"This is a funny, fantastic place," Nicky laughed.

"Woof-onderful!" Harry agreed.

Nicky and Harry spent the
afternoon playing together. First
they played fetch with
snowballs, then they chased
each other and Nicky didn't get
cold once. She didn't even get
the slightest bit chilly, even
though the snow kept falling

46

and she was only wearing a
jumper and shorts and her
trainers. And it didn't matter
how far or how fast they ran,
they never ran into the sides of
the dome. In fact, Nicky
couldn't even see the sides of the
dome.

I must be very, very small,
Nicky thought to herself. Funny,
but I don't feel small. In fact, just
the opposite. Now she had a
friend, she felt like a giant!

After that, they made angels
in the snow. Nicky lay on her
back and moved her arms up

and down at her sides so she
could make the pattern of wings
and Harry lay on his front and
moved his front paws up and
down. Nicky couldn't remember
when she'd had so much fun.
Having a dog was just as she'd
imagined it.

"Nicky, you'd better think about getting back. Your grandad will be wondering where you are," Harry pointed out.

Nicky couldn't bear it. "Oh, Harry! I can come back and play with you again, can't I?"

"Of course you can." Harry  wagged his tail. "And I'll be right here waiting for you."

Nicky picked up Harry and cuddled him. "Oh, it's not fair. I wish you could come out of this dome and be with me."

Oh dear! The snow began to whirl around them faster and faster and it

began to snow *upwards* instead of downwards.

"What's going on?" Nicky called out.

And before she could say another word, she was back in her garden with the snow dome on the grass at her feet and the sun blazing down on her back. And Harry had grown to the size of a real dog and he was standing right in front of her, his golden brown fur and silver paws gleaming in the sun.

"The wish came true." Nicky clapped her hands. "It must be something to do with the rainbow clay. It's made all my wishes come true. Now you can be with me always and for ever and we'll never . . ."

"Nicky, I don't feel well . . ." Harry began, before his voice trailed off altogether. Something was wrong. Harry was in trouble.

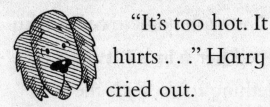 "It's too hot. It hurts . . ." Harry cried out.

And horrified, Nicky watched as Harry's golden fur began to bubble like overheated porridge. And the silver fur of his paws began to chip and flake, fluttering like moonlit rain onto the grass below.

Chapter Four
The Final Wish

"No! Harry, no!" Nicky knelt
down in front of Harry to try
and protect him from the sun's
rays but it was no good. A tiny
crack, no
thicker than
a hair,
appeared
on one of
his ears. He
was starting to
crumble.

"I can't stay here. It's too hot for me," Harry gasped.

"Quick! You've got to go back into the snow dome," Nicky said urgently.

"How?" asked Harry. "I don't know how I came *out* of the dome, so I certainly don't know how to get back in."

Nicky thought desperately.

"I wished it," Nicky realized. "I wished you would leave the dome and be with me for always."

"If you don't *un*wish it and soon, there'll be nothing left of me but dust!" Harry said, lying down. The gold of his fur was flaking faster now. Nicky had to do something. She *had* to. She picked up the dome and held it tightly in both hands.

"Harry, I want you to stay with me so much but not if it's going to make you ill or fall to pieces, so I wish you were back in the dome where you'll be cold and safe and happy."

Before Nicky could blink, Harry had disappeared.

"Harry? Harry, are you in there? Are you OK?" Nicky held the snow dome up to her face and shook it frantically. "Harry?"

"Ah! That's much better," Harry barked happily. He ran around in circles chasing his wagging tail.

"Oh Harry, thank goodness. I'm so glad you're safe." Nicky grinned with relief.

"Nicky, come in for your lunch," called Grandad from the kitchen door.

Nicky leapt to her feet, still holding the snow dome in her hands. "Grandad, did you see . . . ?"

"Shush! I don't want anyone to know that I'm real, except you," said Harry.

"Did I see what?" Grandad prompted.

"Nothing!" Nicky shook her head, hiding her snow dome behind her back.

"Come in now, dear," said Grandad.

"I'll be right there." Nicky waited until Grandad disappeared back into the house before she turned to Harry. "Harry, I've just thought of something," she said.

"If I'm out here and you're in there, how will we play together again? Will I be able to get back into the dome and be with you?"

"If you hold onto the dome with both hands and really, really wish for it to happen, then it will," said Harry.

"D'you think so?" said Nicky anxiously. "You don't think all your rainbow clay magic is used up yet?"

"Nicky, I'm not the only one who's magic," Harry laughed. "Didn't you know that you are too?"

"Me?" asked Nicky, amazed.

"You!" said Harry.

And then Nicky understood.
"So it's not the rainbow clay that's
magic, is it? It's you and me –
together."

"Exactly." And Harry started
chasing his tail again.

Nicky laughed. "Harry, you and I are going to have such fun together."

"Of course we are!" said Harry.

"It's going to be woof-onderful!" said Nicky and Harry together.

And laughing, Nicky carried Harry back into her house. It was time for lunch!

THE END